SHEEPLAND

A PORTRAIT OF THE LIFE OF SHEEP

DR. KAMEL S. ABU JABER

SHEEPLAND

A PORTRAIT OF THE LIFE OF SHEEP

DR. KAMEL S. ABU JABER

HESPERUS

Published by Hesperus Press Limited
www.hesperus.press

First Published by Hesperus Press Limited, 2004
Second Edition Published by Hesperus Press Limited, 2021

Designed and typeset by Roland Codd

ISBN 9781843919834
ebook ISBN 9781843919841

CONTENTS

THE PROCESSION

The Shepherd, lonely,
And his Mount the Mule,
Chief ram and rams,
And ewes and lambs,
Are marching down
The street of life;
The thinking goats
Challenge, disrupt,
And roam around;
The ever-present dogs,
Mongrel and pedigree,
Barking. Keeping order.
The procession of sheep in Sheepland.

EDITOR'S NOTE TO THE SECOND EDITION

In loving memory of my husband
Kamel S. Abu Jaber
1932-2020
Beloved husband, father, grandfather, professor

I am having Dr. Kamel's Sheepland, a satirical essay, written with
characteristic wit and humor, on the state of sheep, through out the ages,
"wherever their pasture," in honor of the 100th anniversary of Jordan,
his beloved country which he served loyally and faithfully
throughout his lifetime.
His devoted wife of 62 years, Loretta.

I am grateful to Hesperus Press for making this possible in these difficult
times and I look forward to working with them in the future in the
publication of Dr. Kamel's other books: *The Palestinians: People of the Olive Tree*,
The Arab Ba'ath Socialist Party: History, Ideology, Organization and *Memoirs*.

"Of Sheep and Shepherds in the Time of Trump" was written by the author
and published in the Opinion Section of *The Jordan Times*, 13 August 2018.
In view of its pertinence to the theme of the book, I thought it
appropriate to have it republished here.

"To the sheep, lambs, ewes and rams, goats, mules, dogs and
Shepherds wherever their pasture."[*]

*For my family; my wife Loretta,
my daughters Linda and Nyla,
my grandchildren, Kamil and Nour-Marie,
Summer-Anne and Abigail, with Love*

[*]This essay is pure fiction. Any resemblance to shepherds, rams, sheep, goats,
mules or dogs, living or dead, is purely coincidental.

SHEEPLAND

INTRODUCTION

In this allegorical essay, truth, fiction and myth are intertwined in exactly the same proportion that exists in the real life of the average human being. That is why imagination and understanding are needed in its reading more than pedantic erudition.

This essay is an analytical description of the life of the ordinary person wherever he may be. In spite of the emphasis on Third World societies, one must remember the flat assertion made by Jean-Jacques Rousseau that "Man is born free, and everywhere he is in chains." To the mind of this author, no ideology – whether religious or secular – has truly freed man from the web of organized society in a state. Like sheep, most human beings, wherever they live, are entrapped by socioeconomic and political forces they do not understand, fathom, or have control over.

Mostly, the tethers that keep man or sheep in their situation are unseen. In current times the pipes and drums of the modern mass media have been added to the effective yet unwritten tripartite concordat between the political, religious and social establishments to maintain control. It is a historical determinism much stronger and more durable than the simplistic economic determinism of Karl Marx. It is an opium that is vastly more pervasive than religion, producing a numbness and apathy that soaks into every pore and every nook and cranny of sheep or men; a condition that most accept.

Conditioned as they are, few dare cross the line of the circle drawn around them. Those who do, pay dearly, and mostly by the terror of the street as well as that of organized society. What often seems to be chaos is really no more than mere randomness, which aims above all to restore the equilibrium of organized society.

Fear, more than anything else, is what keeps order; and the combination of the three establishments – the state, religion and the social order – with its emphasis on rhythmic tradition and motion, is the greatest instiller of fear in man or sheep. Even the most vicious animals can be conditioned to behave and even to perform in a manner designed to please the master: the state. The Shepherd, becomes the changer, the sustainer, the giver, the taker, and the guide. Rewards as well as punishments are his to mete out. For the state is, like God, the only social institution that can provide or withhold liberty; and more importantly, it is the only social institution that can take life whenever the rules it has laid down are broken. No wonder then the pharaoh became Pharaoh, the personification of a living God. And no wonder that later shepherds claimed Divine Right, with one French Shepherd calling himself the Sun King. All was and remains designed to strike fear in the heart of the flock, and to condition them to obey. The taming is not only of the body, but of the mind too.

Not only does the state have control over each and every individual mind, body, and soul, it exercises the same over the life of the entire society. Only the state can change the direction of the entire social order in every facet of life, physical, mental and spiritual. The most dramatic example of such a phenomenon took place when the Soviet Union collapsed and was replaced by what exists now.

The State, damn the State that keeps and maintains the necessary fetters that drive anarchy away!

*   *   *

This symbolic description of some aspects of the life, organization and behavior of the sheep in the world, and in particular in the developing countries, deserves some attention. Sheepland is vast in terms of space and time. It is more or less a conditioned mental attitude having no real boundaries. What made sheep sheep is a question that is only partly answered in the chilly double negative parody related here. Also it is difficult to separate sheep from themselves. From the general to the particular is not only a quantum leap that cannot be made here, it is also an impossible task made more difficult by the docility of the sheep themselves. Sheep would rather live than fight. In Tunisheepia, a pasture called the 'Green' a sheepular saying depicting utter desperation goes, "Who am I but a mere blade of grass that only yearns to survive." If faced with a choice, they would choose what the Shepherd and his dogs want. That is why it is difficult to write about sheep and why so little has been written about them, Surely, everyone knows that history is not the history of sheep but the history of Shepherds and dogs, and their exploits.

Whether in Srisheepia, Argensheepia or Malisheepia, or other similar pastures in Sheepland, sheep share the same basic characteristics and undergo the same type of life related here.

15

"All sheep are shorn by their Shepherd," is a sheepular saying ultimately depicting the unshapely situation of sheep. Judging from the vantage point of our sheep, society is described as a procession. A procession of historical proportions headed by the Shepherd; his mount; the Mirya', or chief ram, called in English the bellwether; other prominent rams; the sheep themselves; the few black goats scattered on the horizons of the flock; and the whole procession flanked by the barking, ever vigilant dogs. As for the mount, the mule – being a romantic if stolid animal, symbolically a dropout from the class above or a climber from the one below – has been chosen. When asked who is his father, a 'proper' mule from Arabisheepia would proudly, if evasively, answer that his uncle is the horse.

This essay is both light and heavy reading. In either case it should be contemplated, meditated on and enjoyed. For that to happen, it is the author's hope that it will be read in installments; a chapter at a time on several quiet afternoons. The reader is asked not to dive too deeply, or swim too quickly, but to drift gently with the current. If you must be critical, remember that the author is an aspiring, anticipating goat, who would like to recall the memory of al-Jahiz and Ibn al-Muqaffa, both of whom perished while out of favor with their contemporary Shepherd. Can anybody ever please the Shepherd in his, of necessity, lonely post?

The allegory was a necessity dictated by the circumstances of life, especially in the Third World. What happened to the lofty hopes and aspirations of the once colonized peoples of the world? Are they better off now with their native leaders and governments?

While this essay may seem at times amusing, it might leave the sensitive reader with a heavy heart. It offers no reasons why things turned out the way they did, nor does it offer a solution for the future. It merely describes, leaving the reader's imagination to its own devices.

SHEEPLAND

If Sheepland were a mythological conception it would not lie as it does on the borders of reality; in that twilight zone between total darkness and the bare flickering of light. Movement suggests that it is not a non-entity not occupying a non-dimension of space. Sadly, Sheepland is a reality, its flocks, Shepherds, and other beasts portraying human development and retardation both at the same time; the zenith and the nadir. Spatially and numerically, Sheepland encompasses most of the known areas of the world. Some observers emphasize that even in non-sheep areas, areas considered more developed, there are sheep flocks and 'sheepish' behavior. These observers add that, historically, most civilizations were built around sheep; that the present technology gap between sheep and so-called non-sheep areas is only a very recent phenomenon; and that, even in the latter areas, sheep do exist and are exploited just as much, albeit in different, perhaps less obvious ways altogether.

It is not our concern to argue the merits or demerits of the case. Nor is it of great concern where sheep are milked and fleeced the most. Surely it is recognized that no one protects sheep interests but the sheep themselves; whether they have failed to protect themselves adequately is another question. Some observers, however – in particular one Ortega-sheep – argue that the masses of sheep care little about what is happening to them, and that most sheep go through life without heeding the dangers they are subjected to or the abuse they undergo.

Most sheep, argues another well-known sheepologist, are 'other directed' anyway. Perhaps that is why they survive. It is argued by some that should sheep wish to survive indefinitely, they must evolve smaller bodies. These observers put forward the tangential argument that this is how ants and bees survived and developed a harmonious social order; however they overlook two very important limitations on sheep. The first is that Shepherds will not permit sheep to develop in any way except that which proves beneficial to the Shepherds themselves. In essence, there is a basic contradiction between the Shepherd and his sheep. The Shepherd is keen on having his sheep fatter and with bigger bodies and woollier, never mind about the harmoniousness of their social behavior or, for that matter, their very survival. The second is that the Shepherd has, over the years, convinced the sheep themselves that they exist to make him happy. Making him happy means that they have to develop larger bodies, not smaller, and the argument goes on and on and on.

Surely the sheep are aware of the threats, subtly advanced by their Shepherd on certain occasions, to the effect that he will develop alternative beasts. It is a rare sheep that does not happily bleat when the Shepherd appears. Sheep are constantly reminded of the love and care of their Shepherd and how worried he was one day when he lost one of his lambs. The story of the Prodigal Lamb has become a byword among sheep explicating the true love of the Shepherd for every sheep in his flock.

Throughout history, many young lambs have put forward arguments against Shepherds. Treatises and seminars and schools of sheep-thought have arisen to delineate the contours of his authority. No sooner is one Shepherd in, than the flock discovers he is barely any different from the previous one. In modern times several factors account for this development, not the least of which is the rise of Charismatic Shepherds, aided, of course, by modern technology in the field of mass media.

Sheepulation growth and certain historical cultural factors and social practices, in addition to demands by the sheep themselves for welfare services, have made the rise of the authoritarian administration – and in some rural areas of Sheepland, even totalitarian practices and styles of administration – very much in vogue.

In fact, though this is a digression of sorts, some Shepherds have been known to boast about the docility, meekness and (as some observers would even derisively say) *sheepishness* of their flocks. It has been observed that in some areas of Sheepland, the more docile the flock, the more vicious the Shepherd becomes. In ancient times one Shepherd called Juliusheep Caesar put the blame squarely on the backs of the sheep. Elevating his sheep to the status of citizens, he said, "Corrupt citizens breed corrupt rulers and it is the mob that decides when virtue shall die." No sheep has ever contested this statement, which could, after all, be true. No one knows for sure, although one late nineteenth-century sheepologist by the name of Scapegoat remarked on a truism of his age, "It is always dangerous to speak the truth in a corrupt society."

Maybe this is true of all ages, especially when one remembers the Roman dictum, "Corruptio, optimi, pessima," (power corrupts the best) or the saying of the nineteenth-century Britisheepia Lord Ram-Acton, "Power corrupts, and absolute power corrupts absolutely."

Some illustrative examples may be useful at this stage. Most sheep, even illiterate ones, must still recall the happenings involving a Shepherd called Bucasaram. He became so preoccupied with acquiring more titles and powers to himself that even his own sheep became upset and reacted by trampling him. Only his vast gold throne remains in the pen, which his sheep still inhabit. Later, it was discovered that he had mortgaged his sheep's wool and milk for many, many years to come without even telling his Mirya' or any of his chief rams.

Another incident involving a Shepherd from a rural area of Sheepland called Afrisheepia was more spectacular, bizarre and startling. Here the sheep were so upset that they arose en masse and ran their Shepherd out of their pen. It was documented later that this Idiram specialized in mass killings. Certain categories of his sheep ran away and became 'refusheep' in neighboring pastures. It was discovered that he almost annihilated the few goats of his flock. The Shepherd that followed him, having himself elected with the help of a neighboring area's Shepherd and his dogs, has shown pictures of the cruelties of the ousted Shepherd. Another Shepherd, who sent many of his rams to the butcher, when asked about it, replied that these rams were developing some Shepherd-like characteristics that were not healthy for them; and that, had he not dispatched them so quickly, chaos would have ensued within the flock. It was at best a confused argument that further confused his sheep, but it worked. Very soon this particular Shepherd got his major rams involved in a lengthy and exhausting butting match with the rams of a neighboring pasture. No sooner had that eight-year butting match come to a close than this Shepherd proceeded to occupy a small pasture next door with exceedingly fat and woolly sheep nourished by an oily substance extracted from the ground. A ram from the only remaining Super Pasture in the world, and who helped instigate both conflicts, was quoted as saying – while the first conflict was still in progress – that he hoped both Shepherds would lose.

The occupation of the mini-pasture gave the Super Shepherd cause to feign indignation at the umbrage of the local Shepherd for occupying this particular oily pasture. And though strong rumors circulated that the whole affair was engineered by his underground Central Sniffing Agency, the Super Shepherd, who once circulated the slogan that he 'would work for a gentler world', was swift in getting the Shepherds of every western pasture to gang up on and oust the errant Shepherd from the mini-pasture. Over a decade later most of these same western Shepherds ganged up again, this time to dethrone this Irakisheepia Shepherd, under the guise that he was cruel to his own sheep and that he could not be allowed to control the nourishing black juice under the ground of his own pasture. Incidentally almost all the local Shepherds in the area of conflict cooperated in ousting their fellow Shepherd, which angered and further frustrated their own sheep. This area, Arabisheepia, noted for instability, has developed some of the most colorful and romantic names for its various pastures and their Shepherds.

Regardless of the names, however, all have as their backbone the support of their local sniffer dogs. Sadly, to outsiders, the idea of a resheeplic, imported from the western pastures, has metamorphosed in Kafkaesque style into a hereditary system devoted to exalting their Shepherd. It is here where one of the local Shepherds, in attempting to appear to identify with his sheep, invented the name sheepahiriyeh (Jamahiriyeh), a name never before known to beast or man. It is in this region too that one major Shepherd, in attempting to appear more sheepocratic, stated that if his sheep wanted to choose their Shepherd sheepocratically, they could choose from one of his two male offspring.

Incidents like these could be multiplied for illustration. Suffice it to say that the sheep are somehow never wise to the Shepherds' scheming and tricks. One reason is that Shepherds maintain the form, if not the essence, of consulting with their sheep through councils or similar bodies, sometimes elections, mostly rigged in favor of the Shepherd, or one of his favorite dogs or rams; sometimes sheepicites. It has been observed that no Shepherd in Sheepland, in recent decades, has lost an election or a sheepicite, Mostly they win with high majorities, often reaching 99.9% of the vote. While it speaks well for the strategy and tactics of the Shepherd as well as the devotion of his sheep, no one has ever figured out what happens to the small minority of votes against, or what it represents or why. Some observers think that the negative vote must represent the opinion of the goats. No one knows for sure. Such happenings are not unheard of even in the North pastures. In a recent election in the Super Pasture, the Shepherd who lost the sheepular vote was made Shepherd-in-Chief by a decision in his favor by the highest court of his pasture.

Incidentally, Bucasaram never bothered to have himself voted in. Some observers think that is why he was ousted; for having sinned against current etiquette and form. Others think he was too honest with his sheep when he told them he really did not care how they think, what they think of him, or whether they think at all!

Incidents like those cited, however, are rare and are getting rarer. Reasons are many and too difficult, if not superfluous, to catalogue. Chief among these reasons, however, is the fact that the Shepherds have appreciably increased the number of dogs in their pastures. This is curious since the Shepherds must be aware, as every sheep is aware, that sheep never catch on, nor do they acquire wisdom or experience with age. Surely no one expects sheep to benefit from history; that is, even if they know it at all.

Outsiders, mostly foreign experts who come for brief visits to some areas of Sheepland, know that the sheep are unaware. At a glance they can size-up the situation, identifying that while there is some deference to form, the essence is missing; and that, while in some cases you can see prosperity among certain classes of sheep, there is in fact no hope. From the sheep's droopy, limpid, almost always watery eyes, these experts can tell there is no hope and yet there is no danger to the Shepherd. That is why some of them wonder why the Shepherd worries to such an extent that he is constantly increasing the number of his dogs.

No doubt the 'technology transfer' has been most efficacious in spheres of mass sheepulation, mass control and listening and eavesdropping devices. That is why, wherever you go in Sheepland, the locals will caution you concerning the efficiency of their local Kennel. Some sheep, even those who have previously suffered at the hands of their local Kennel, will proudly, although vicariously and masochistically, point to its efficiency. This efficiency is continuously supplemented by the importation of new techniques, new pedigree breeds of dogs from abroad, or through the development of new local pedigrees. Some experts in canine behavior speak with wonderment about the apparent unity of purpose existing among almost all the Kennels of Sheepland. In one part of Sheepland, an area noted for disarray and lacking a spirit of cooperation in most aspects of life among its Shepherds, there exists one exception: cooperation on security matters of the regional sniffers. This is as if to prove that the Shepherd and his sheep live in close geographical proximity. They in fact, are worlds apart; in two different universes altogether.

The development of the Kennel is viewed with a certain amount of apprehension, even sadness in certain quarters. Some sheepologists argue convincingly that such develop-ments are psychologically – and even socially and politically – damaging to sheep. Eventually their spirit gets broken, they give less and less milk, and soon become too lean and their wool too brittle. Even fleecing them becomes very difficult, though not impossible.

Viewed from the Shepherd's angle, however, these developments do not seem to be unwelcome. Shepherds, or shepherdophiles, spread the word that stability in the pasture is more valuable than anything else in life. One Hobbesram, a seventeenth century politico-sheepologist of note, argued that without stability you cannot have fatter and happier sheep; nor will the meadows, for that matter, produce enough fodder. Stability is the essence, this sheepelectual argued. Without it, a sheep's life will be "nasty, brutish, and short." Some others argue that, ultimately, since there must be a Shepherd anyway, why not this particular one? Almost a convincing argument, although some Shepherds get carried away with it.

To the udder chagrin of the sheep, technology has developed in a most degrading manner where even their milking is done by automatic milking machines without the simplest touch of a human hand. Moreover, most sheep are increasingly known by numbers assigned to them, visibly displayed on ID cards on their chests or, in some cases, tagged elsewhere on their bodies.

Technology, no doubt, has been a great help to Shepherds with hardly a pasture that does not have its own local radio and television station. Notice that we are not speaking of proper or appropriate technologies. In some of the rural areas of Sheepland, for instance, the Shepherd may become very proud and boast about the traffic lights he installed at intersections; a bit silly though understandable, in spite of the fact that sheep traffic can very often be regulated more efficiently by dogs, considering their stage of development. But that is how it is anyway. Returning to the topic of radio and television, these specialize mainly in extolling the virtues of the Shepherd through songs, dances and sheeplore exhibitions. The Shepherd is somehow always linked to earlier glorious developments or achievements in the history of his particular flock. Many observers wonder at the inventiveness of these programs which is not present elsewhere in other aspects of the life of the flock; how they can make a small achievement into a major one, and so convincingly that even the skeptical sheep eventually begin to believe it, 'wonder of wonders'. Perhaps it is the constant repetition that makes an illusory or outlandish incident seem familiar. These innovative tendencies are appreciated mostly by the Shepherd, who often helps in inventing historical occasions. The Shepherd is always given ample time to communicate his ideas, his musical sessions becoming state affairs. It is, nowadays, almost a requirement that a 'good' Shepherd, or at least an efficient one, plays some type of musical instrument, ranging from the simple, ancient flute to more modern and perhaps even radical instruments. One scandalous Super Shepherd was famous for playing fine tunes for his sheep on the saxophone. Some supposed he was trying to look sheepish with his sheep.

In their musical sessions some Shepherds have developed certain very sophisticated concepts for the ideology of their administration. Regardless of how progressive a Shepherd may be, most of them find traditional music very useful and soothing to the nature of sheep: Even blue-eyed Shepherds with fair hair hark back to this type of music once in a while. In most of Sheepland, however, and regardless of the name the Shepherd gives his type of music, it is really, at best, an eclectic, sophisticated or semi-sophisticated hybrid. Often the medley is a cacophonous orchestration of unrelated sounds. 'Negritude' for black sheep or a 'Pan' in Arabisheepia, Latin Ameisheepia or Asiasheepia these musical tunes advanced by the Shepherds share some things in common. They are firstly an emotional medley, most concerned with stability while giving the illusion of egalitarianism, and finally promising to improve the welfare and quality of life of sheep. The tunes usually play on the anti-wolf sentiments of their sheep, hoping to keep their area of Sheepland separate from wolfish struggles elsewhere. Incidentally, the 'big bad wolves' do not seem to mind this fabricated separation and in fact encourage it, often sending observers to interpastural Shepherd gatherings to help in the passing of long-winded resolutions.

The most sustained and effective trick the Shepherds use for making their sheep believe in their music is the constant repetition of ramiotic tunes. While in the beginning some of the sheep used to resent these constant and repetitious musical sessions, eventually they became part of their daily existence, the ideas filtering in without the conscious awareness of the sheep. In the end the Shepherds themselves began to believe their own tunes, which is very dangerous. You see, when they reach that stage two things may happen: first, the dogs begin to believe too and get lulled to sleep, thus paving the way for other Shepherds to arise in the flock; or secondly, some of the dogs may enter into a state of amnesia, forgetting who they are or what their function is, and beginning to think they can do what the Shepherd is doing and maybe more efficiently, Since they were all in it together – that is, they themselves and the Shepherd – some of these dogs eventually help in the rise of other Shepherds. Dogs are never at a loss to find goats and sheep renegades who will help them, shortsightedly of course, against their Shepherd.

It would seem that Sheepland could continue in this state of affairs for a long time to come. What with its own internal insecurities and uncertainties, in addition to the machinations of the 'big bad wolves', no serious sheepologist is prepared to predict a happier or more stable order. For even if and when sheep are, once in a while, deferred to by their Shepherd, they know, deep down in their ruminations, that they can always be blamed by him for one thing or another. One of the most recent preposterous accusations against them was that their flatulence – in a pasture called Australisheepia – was a major cause for the hole in the ozone, causing global warming. So it seems that Sheepland is likely destined to remain in that twilight zone between light and darkness, mentioned earlier.

THE SHEEP

Anyone who has ever roamed the countryside of any developing country must be struck by the great inequality, and yet the seeming serenity prevalent among the sheep. They appear so serene that they look 'sheepish'. That is why it is difficult to imagine a situation where peace may not be a reality between sheep and others. The sheep is a four legged woolly animal that is blessed by God; the more so because of its seeming peacefulness, lack of reaction, and total acceptance of whatever happens to it. Sheep never act, and rarely react unless frightened, and when frightened their reaction is usually disorganized and without direction. The Shepherd of course is keen on scaring them every so often. This is to keep them further off balance and to increase their reliance and dependence on him at all times. These scare tactics at the same time keep their eyes away from what is really happening to them. To the Shepherd, his priority and what matters is their total obedience and submission. The coupling of the word 'shep', a contraction of the word sheep, with that of 'herd' is not accidental. The word 'herd' carries with it derogatory nuances suggestive of a conformist mentality and a strong attachment to mediocrity. The Shepherd prefers those around him to be mediocre, especially those holding senior positions. They are more obedient and easier to manipulate that way.

No sheep has ever been known to be capable of abstract thinking, though many of them have romantic natures with an infinite capacity, at times, for heroism. Why not, since in almost all religions and creeds they are referred to with reverence, or even awe. Abraham, father of the three great monotheistic religions, was ordered to sacrifice a male sheep, a ram, instead of his son Isaac; in addition there are numerous references to the Lamb of God, and almost all great painters, poets, and even political thinkers resort to using the image of sheep as their subjects. Again this is not to ewelogise the sheep but to put them where they belong in the Saga of life.

Sheep by definition, and in peaceful times, are well organized – or seem to be – their organization being highly centralized and hierarchical following their Shepherd. A Shepherd is one who tends and leads sheep. In his hand the Shepherd usually brandishes a staff, which in addition to its other uses symbolizes his authority. To help him in regulating the affairs of the flock, (sheep society) the Shepherd has usually developed certain methods for better controlling his flock. He plays them certain types of music to which the sheep always react favorably. In fact most sheep bleat favorably when hearing the tunes of the Shepherd, regardless of how many times he repeats them. The Shepherd knows their romantic and nostalgic nature quite well. He knows that while their heads are down they look backward at the same time. They seem to be more comfortable in the grip of tradition. They like to bleat in clichés, their bleats peppered with platitudes, proverbs, and sheepular sayings that save them from thinking situations through. To please their Shepherd, they are prone to respond to his queries the way they think he wants them to. That is why the Shepherd appears to communicate with them in clichés.

Shepherd music is necessary for the welfare and fattening of the flock. In fact their fleece seems to shine and sparkle after such sessions. At such times, their eyes shine as if in expectant anticipation,.

It is not uncommon for the Shepherd to play traditional music thus drawing sheep's attention to their glorious past. Many sheep like this kind of music and they seem to give better and more milk that evening. It reminds them of the greatness of their pasture. Other groups in the flock demand other types of music. This is especially true among the young lambs and kids whose expectations of life seem to be different. For these, the Shepherd usually plays special tunes. In some cases, and in some flocks, if they threaten to become too troublesome, they get isolated from the flock or even sold to butchers. It is ironic that young lambs always dream of a better life and it is ironic also that they never learn to accept their lot. For them, as well as for the benefit of older members of the flock, the Shepherd often resorts to looking pious: visibly praying, sometimes growing a beard, or ostentatiously brandishing a prayer book or beads. Moreover, his musical sessions are often liberally salted with religious sayings and exhortations.

For better control of the flock, the Shepherd solicits the help of certain types of dogs. These dogs are so trained by the Shepherd that often they are more faithful to him than he appears to be to himself. They are so well trained that they seem to appreciate and anticipate every whim of the Master even before he spells it out. They often seem to smell his desires even before he thinks them out. And because they are so close to the sheep themselves, often sleeping in the same pens with them, they are crueler to the sheep than the Master is. Unlike him, they cannot afford to be merciful. Some observers think this is quite curious and sinister, since the saying 'wild and woolly' has never been used with reference to sheep.

To further his control of the flock, the Shepherd even trains some of the sheep themselves to become part of his administration. Of several lambs usually chosen for such a task, one is selected as a Mirya' leader, the others are held in reserve. Of course the Shepherd has seen certain traits in this young lamb. He should look as if he has virility, aggressiveness combativeness and a certain amount of cruelty. Carefully fed on a special diet, this young lamb (and the others in reserve) soon develops a huge body, much larger than the other lambs in the flock. He also soon develops huge horns that the Shepherd often sharpens for him. You see, this helps him in dominating the rams in the flock, and usually he becomes the idol of all the ewes, although most ewes do not know why. For further distinction, the Shepherd dyes his fleece a different color from that of the rest of the flock. This Mirya', as this sheep leader is called in Arabisheepia, is always close to the Shepherd and his mount. In fact, in the procession of the flock, the Shepherd is usually followed by his mount, a mule or a donkey, and then immediately by the Mirya'. To further distinguish the Mirya', a huge bell is often hung around his neck, emitting slow, monotonous sounds that help in regulating the step of the sheep. The dogs, flanking the flock, keep the sheep in line, intimidating the rebellious and maintaining the order of the procession; while the few goats and their billy goat who is usualy accompanying the flock, wander about in their usual disorderly fashion, generally not heeding the barking dogs.

It is well to remember that the sheep, under these circumstances, rarely if ever react. Truly, they rarely even react unless totally frightened or in alien surroundings. The Shepherd loves or appears to love his sheep. This is why he keeps them so well organized and under complete control, and why he has to think for them, and why he rarely, if ever, consults with them.

All of that which he does, he says is for their own good. He emphasizes to them, as well as to other flocks in neighboring pastures, that he is always at their service, sacrificing his sleep and rest for their benefit and protection. He tells them that his love for them knows no bounds and that this is why he has to remain in control, so that he can prevent other Shepherds form causing them harm.

The sheep are always alert to possible conspiracies and would-be conspirators; and because of their accepting nature, they believe what they hear. No sheep has ever arisen to tell them otherwise, and other Shepherds always seem to be doing less for their flocks than their own. They grow to love their Shepherd and believe everything he tells them in his musical sessions. With such short memories, most sheep never realize whether they are happy or not. They muddle through life not realizing the dangers that exist to their lives. Only when a close sheep is dragged to the butcher or killed before their eyes, do they realize their desperate situation; yet even in those cases, for only a short time.

The Shepherd reminds them also of the ever-present wolves constantly prowling around hoping to attack Sheepland. It is true that the wolves have a record of aggression, and it is also true that the wolves are merciless. Yet some sheep often wonder whether the price they pay is a bit high. The sheep never question the fleecing, the milking, even the beatings and punishments that their Shepherd administers to some of them. Yet sometimes they wonder why it is that no one is worrying about their opinions, or consulting with them on any very vital sheeply matters; matters that concern their very flesh and wool.

Sheep of color, or colored sheep, not only cannot escape the attention of the Shepherd, they cannot even escape the negative attention of the other sheep who like to keep their distance. These have nothing to do with the so-called 'black sheep' who are really white but called black because for the moment they are out of favor with their Shepherd, or are in trouble with him for one reason or another. Black or colored sheep have discovered that though they have been 'emancipated' at one time or another by worthy Shepherds with lofty ideals, in fact they never seem able to make it as equals to their so-called brethren the white sheep. Though the only thing they share with the goats is the color black – which also means they cannot hide from the Shepherd, his dogs or even the ordinary sheep themselves – like the goats, they too are always candidates for one type of trouble or another. Anyway, colored sheep are held in such disdain that any sheep, whatever color it may be, is referred to as the black sheep of the family, when it has fallen into disfavor.

THE SHEPHERD

No one knows for sure where Shepherds got their mandate to be Shepherds, nor for that matter the origin of that mandate. In ancient times some Shepherds claimed they were Gods incarnate; later, only that they were the 'shadow of God', and then, much later, only that their mandate came from God. Nowadays, no sheep takes these arguments seriously, recognizing that they only benefit the Shepherds. Some theories have arisen limiting the powers of Shepherds, and in some of the western pastures Shepherds' powers are, in fact, limited drastically. Rural, eastern and southern Shepherds have been known to emulate in form, though not in fact, Shepherds' behavior in the western ranges. No one here, however, is fooled. Not even the sheep that shake their hands knowingly and sometimes even sagely. Here, most Shepherds like to appear 'elected' though some inherit their positions.

The 'elections' are in fact only sheepicites where the name of only one candidate appears on the ballots, with the result of astounding majorities reaching as high as 99.9% of the votes cast. In his last election before being ousted by the Shepherd of the only Super Pasture, one local Shepherd – whose name means the 'butter', and whose pasture smelled of fatty black oil coveted by the Super Shepherd received a 100% majority. When the sheep in an Arabisheepia pasture demanded to be given a real choice, their Shepherd was heard to remark that he thought it was a reasonable request and that they could choose one of his two male siblings – only after his demise, of course, and never mind the supposedly resheeplican form of government.

Shepherds have been happy to have their sheep acquire only a little knowledge and a few skills – but only some, and very limited ones. They teach their sheep, or rather inculcate in their sheep, the habit of not thinking clearly. One Shepherd was once heard to remark that, "a good sheep is a dumb one," while another Shepherd was quoted as saying that, "you should never let your flock know the truth." It is better, he said, "if the truth remains obfuscated and if the sheep remain unaware." That is why most flocks are taught to walk around in a procession with their heads hanging down and their eyes looking backward. Sheep are taught by the Shepherd to be inhibited, never expressing an opinion in public without hesitation or stuttering. Most Shepherds inculcate in the flock the concept of shame, and that is why most sheep think it vulgar to assert their rights or to express an opinion. They are taught to defer to rams, older sheep or older ewes; never to stray, if possible, from the trodden path; and never to become too visibly successful. A sheepular saying in the southern pastures goes, "Put your head among other heads and hope never to be noticed."

Ram or even sheep success is not very well encouraged or accepted in Sheepland. In fact, it has been advanced by some ramologists that the sheep that survives is the one that successfully and proudly keeps its head down, never coming to the notice of the Shepherd. One notable Shepherd was once heard to remark, "It is a happy sheep which is away from the notice of the Shepherd." One of the most learned, just, and historically famous Shepherds in Arabisheepia, who was given the title of 'the Entrusted', was once heard to say, "The Sultan is he whom I do not know, and he in turn does not know me." Of course all sheep recall the injunction of all ewes to their lambs, "Never walk immediately behind a Mule or in front of a Shepherd." – for obvious reason. Success, these ramologists argue, is visible, whereas failure can always be swept under the rug, or capitalized upon by the Shepherd to blackmail the failing ram or sheep. Success, especially among prominent sheep or rams, is looked upon as a nuisance, because when a ram succeeds he is immediately juxtaposed with the Shepherd or with other more important rams.

A successful ram is one who fails, or makes himself appear to be a failure, by pretending to lose either his memory or some of his skills. Any good idea must appear to come from the Shepherd or be a result of his instructions. Since no one in Sheepland is ever quite sure where his future lies, it is better, most rams publicly argue, to blend in with the rest of the flock. It has not been unknown for some goats or intellectual rams to go to great lengths to blend in with the scenery of the pasture and the flock. Some of them, in recent decades, have taken to taking medications in the form of pills or even suppositories against intelligence, logic and understanding.

Shepherds have become ingenious in their methods of controlling their flocks without seeming to be doing so. In some of the southern pastures, in particular in Arabisheepia, the Shepherds, aware of the fatalistic and traditional nature of their sheep, encourage that seemingly unwritten pact between the educational, the political, and the religious establishments to maintain the mental status quo. The Shepherds here are clearly keen on preventing their sheep from thinking; as if aware that should thinking occur, their own position would become jeopardized. Some flocks are always induced to fright by the Shepherds. Wolves, real or imaginary, are constantly used. Canned wolf sounds and howling are often repeated on radio and television, reminding sheep of what will happen to them should the eye of their Shepherd not be on them constantly. The fact that few sheep can recall any such wolf attack, or that they know wolf existence to be mostly mythological, does not seem to lessen the impact on the Shepherd-sheep relationship. A witty sheepologist once remarked that such a relationship is like an unhappy marriage involving a continuing interaction between both parties, in which the stronger one may not always dominate while at the same time controlling the weaker.

No one would say for sure that Sheepland was ruled through terror tactics alone, or that most Shepherds are not gentle or merciful with their flocks. Ewephemisms aside, however, some would argue there are few concepts or words to describe the situation otherwise. It really depends from pasture to pasture, or from meadow to meadow. In some, naked brute terror is not unheard of; while in others, different methods, appearing more merciful, though by no means less effective, are found. In one area even sheep thought was tampered with; the method was given the ennobling ewephemism of 'brain washing', leading some observes to remark sarcastically "…as if sheep have dirty thoughts!" In fact these observers argue almost convincingly that sheep 'brains' have either been eaten by the Shepherds, his dogs and guests, or that they have been 'drained' by migration, mostly to the western pastures. Most of those that remain have either surrendered completely or are in an advanced stage of alienation anyway.

To convince their sheep, some Shepherds have resorted to issuing small books, which they distribute freely and liberally among their flocks. These little books, produced in bright colors sheepular among certain flocks, contain most of the proper thoughts that decent sheep should think. Shepherds argue that should sheep stick to the axioms, truths and prescriptions contained in these lovely little books, no harm will come to them and there will be no need for the sheep to have their brains contaminated with dirty, alien thoughts. Being superstitious, most sheep in these areas have taken to keeping these little books with them at all times. Like amulets against the evil eye, the sheep have been known to hang them around their necks.

This in not tyranny, Shepherds and shepophiles argue. This emanates from the deep love and affection the Shepherd has for his sheep. Why should sheep bother to think when he can easily think for them and provide them with proper opinions? Some Shepherds argue their case on two sophisticated grounds: first, that thinking sheep age prematurely, thus their meat becomes tough; and secondly, that it is in the tradition of Sheepland anyway to think in terms of clichés and popular sayings. These little books, with their bright colors, are a continuation of the tradition. One Shepherd went so far as to say that, "Tyranny equally distributed among all is in fact justice to all." In dealing with their Shepherds in this area, another saying goes, "Kiss the Shepherd's hand, and yet hope that it be served." Sheep cannot bite.

That is why in most areas of Sheepland most Shepherds keep or try to keep their sheep fragmented – even atomized – never permitting them to congregate except in the procession, and under strict discipline. Most Shepherds believe that ultimately each sheep should account for its own actions, making good their saying that, "Eventually each sheep will end up hanging by its own two hind legs." A gruesome thought that most sheep detest, knowing full well that whether here or in the hereafter, it is true. Shepherds try to keep sheep minds off such matters and some have developed ingenious ways to accomplish that.

Such an ingenious Shepherd, to get the minds of his sheep away from their stagnant conditions, allowed one educated ram to become a jester, poking fun at the abuse of power and the lack of free bleating, and thus providing a sort of mental escape; a catharsis for the flock. This jester's theatricals and plays were so sheepular that even other Shepherds in neighboring pastures used them to cool sheep tempers. Once when this jester visited a friendly flock it was estimated that seventy thousand sheep attended his performances each night, for two consecutive weeks. Sheep-opposition papers as well as sheep-demonstrators bleated their desire that such a jester should arise among them. Incidentally, none did. Sheep of the region enjoyed the theatricals that helped them in venting their frustrations peacefully, while Shepherds of the region thought of it as an inexpensive and effective exercise in containment.

Successful Shepherds, though themselves fond of titles and conspicuous display and consumption, present a different face to their flocks. They always look friendly, fatherly, pious, and as though they adhere to sheep ethics, mores, sensitivities, sensibilities and traditions. It is said, though it is by no means proven, that once a Shepherd begins to flaunt his authority, unheeding of his flocks' sensibilities, he is on his way out of their favor. One Shepherd, who didn't listen to the contrary advice of his neighboring shepherds or the strong bleating reportedly heard among his flock, made peace with some wolves in the neighborhood; an act contrary to all sheeply etiquette, morality and traditions. He was assassinated for it. It brings to mind the popular sheepular saying, "Even some smart Shepherds can sometimes err."

Though some Shepherds do sometimes get heady and carried away, it is only on rare occasions that relations among them are suspended. Though they often ostentatiously cut off sheeplomatic relations, surreptitiously and unbeknownst to their flocks they keep their feelers in touch and their ears to the ground. Shepherds, by and large, and regardless of the tunes they play to their flocks, support each other and try to maintain friendly relations. No sooner does a Shepherd die, get trampled by his sheep – a rare occurrence – or run out by the rams and goats of his area, than the other Shepherds recognize the authority of the subsequent Shepherd with a speed puzzling to most sheep. 'What happened to the love and respect our Shepherd had for the dead or ousted Shepherd?' the sheep wonder. They never, however, know the answer. Instilling in their sheep the virtues of complacency, intellectual lethargy, lack of initiative, the Shepherds usually cooperate closely with each other. It is rare that Shepherds, even if enemies, will attempt to undermine each other. One prominent sheepologist and historian of sheep behavior argues that Shepherds never really like to inflict harm on each other, though at times their dogs may fight. The same historian argues that, in peaceful times, the dogs of different flocks always cooperate even if friendly relations do not appear to prevail among the Shepherds.

On the contrary, Shepherds go to great lengths to maintain friendly relations between their 'peace loving flocks'. Sheep attention is always held through the exchange of Shepherdly, sheeply visits, or through the holding of bilateral or multilateral 'brotherly' conferences held among 'sisterly' flocks which are, needless to say, given prominent publicity. Each Shepherd attending these gatherings prepares a beautiful tune designed as much for his own flock's consumption as for the occasion. Usually they take along with them the Mirya' and some other very prominent rams. If the gathering is held in some progressive area of Sheepland, many Shepherds take with them some of the fatter ewes of the flock.

At home Shepherds, regardless of how gentle or dreamy-eyed they look, are very jealous of their privileges and prerogatives. All of them appear to have studied at the hand of one master. Basically, they seem to adhere to the teachings of one Ramachiavelli who wrote a book dedicated to his Shepherd entitled humbly, *The Shepherd*. In it he advises his master to be all things to all sheep; to speak from both sides of his mouth at the same time, which is no mean feat;

and to do whatever may be necessary to maintain control, "Reaching the end of the road," he states, justifies any means the Shepherd may employ. Though he may not be any of the good things he appears to be, the image he projects is more important than his actual deeds or behavior. Even while committing slaughter he should appear to be doing it for the good of the flock; or, while punishing, he should appear fatherly and merciful. He should look pious, a father and a family man, accompanied to his musical sessions by his siblings and favorite ewes. Committing cruelties in a vulgar manner was taboo, Ramachaivelli added, "If you must be cruel, do all your cruelties at once; not in stages. Sheep forget it faster that way, and. if you pilfer the sheep economy for your use, do it in a subtle, unobtrusive way that the sheep will appreciate. Always, however, appear to be the father of your sheep."

THE RAMS

In the southern ranges, and in the absence of rational means of selection or election, all rams become eligible to hold all offices regardless of talent. It is not by a process of election, nor is it by belonging to a political gathering or school of sheep-thought, but literally by the whim or even whimsy of the Shepherd that some lambs become rams or rams with office, prestige or title. If a lamb escapes the attention of the Shepherd long enough, he stands a good chance of making it to ramhood. With ramhood usually comes a coveted position in the flock, especially among the ewes. In an average flock there usually exist around two dozen rams with elevated positions to help the Mirya' in serving and servicing the flock. Other rams remain in waiting in the hope they may one day be elevated too.

Notwithstanding their present status in Sheepland, depending as it does almost entirely on the will of the Shepherd, historically rams have always stood for something. Worthy of mention is the fact that in ancient times some rams were worshipped and gods were made in their images. The ramhead, Khnum, was the God of Light in the days of the Pharaohs. Along with some species of goats, rams have, despite their diminished status, stood for introducing new ideas. Some might say that along with the goats, they were idea introducers, acting, as it were, as the middle class might in modern times.

In some of the western pastures the Mirya' is usually called the bellwether; a term which makes a lot of sense, since he is distinguished from all of the sheep by having a very large bell hung around his neck emitting slow monotonous sounds that help in regulating the step of the entire flock. In approaching a village or a camp towards the evening it is the bell of the Mirya' that is first heard alerting all to the arrival of the flock.

Whether in ancient times or in the modern era, however, the ram has stood on its hooves, a symbol of virility, fertility, richness, continuity, strength; even obstinacy. Once the God of Light, it has also stood for some enlightenment and some creativity. Historically representing the middle and upper classes in Sheepland, rams were responsible for enterprise while at the same time being conservative. Their conservatism was born out of their sense of duty to maintain the continuity of the social fabric and its mores and ethics. Politically, they almost always sided with Shepherds, adhering to the saying in Arabisheepia, "He who marries my mother becomes my uncle." Only on very rare occasions have rams attempted to upset the status quo.

That is why some observers feel sad and a bit worried at the reduced status of rams in Sheepland nowadays. These observers feel that the rams too are becoming sheepellectually sterile, what with the terrific powers given to the dogs. It is an established fact now that rams are constantly trying to please their Shepherd in any way he may desire instead of functioning as they once did as the spearhead or ramhead introducing innovations. Most rams now are scrambling around to hold certain coveted positions instead of busying themselves with other more fruitful endeavors. Encouraged by the Shepherd, regardless of their individual merits, to vie for his favor, they all feel they are just as entitled as any sheep to hold certain positions. With the Shepherd deliberately setting no standards, and in the absence of form as well as essence to judge by, all rams are 'butting', so to speak, against each other for the very few favors they hope to get from the Shepherd. This is not an unwelcome situation to the Shepherd, incidentally. On the contrary, he feels it is better to keep them busy with each other – providing of course they do not do permanent damage to each other – rather than to have them watching his actions all the time. Remember the sheepular saying, "For the Shepherd even rams are ewes."

Many sheepologists lament these developments, not so much for the condition of the flock alone but for the ultimate damage it eventually does to the Shepherd himself. They feel it is a short-sighted policy on the part of the Shepherd to 'castrate', so to speak, his rams in this way; and this in addition to his encouragement for them to display their possessions so conspicuously and ostentatiously. In most of Sheepland, rams have become preoccupied with displaying their newly acquired possessions, often in a tasteless manner. Some of them build huge corrals with outlandish décor, others dye their favorite ewes' wool with curious imported colors, while still others have taken to conspicuous consumption of certain types of foods and drinks known to be harmful to sheep. This they do for the sake of fad, or fashion.

Lamentable or not, that is the situation prevalent nowadays among the rams in Sheepland. Energies dissipated, milk spilled unnecessarily, and useless displays of wealth that have neither rhyme nor reason. The situation, no doubt momentarily comfortable to the Shepherd and the dogs, is harmful to the flock in the long run. This has led some observers to believe that goats perhaps remain the only group in the flock that may continue to introduce new ideas. A hope, but before discussing its merits it is only fair to discuss the role and status of the chief ram, the Mirya'.

THE MIRYA', THE BELLWETHER

In an earlier discussion, allusion was made to the position and some of the powers and prerogatives of the Mirya', his place in the procession and other aspects of his status. The following remarks will shed further light on his very important position in the life of the flock, as well as the criteria for his selection and the role he is expected to play. Contrary to sheepular imagination, most Mirya's are not selected for their sexual or physical prowess but for their passivity, lethargy and propensity to be led and to accept a secondary position, even though they are expected to lead. If this sounds like a contradiction in terms, well – that is the way it is in Sheepland – the Mirya' must never appear to be too bright. Even if he is, he knows that he must appear to be a leader though in fact he knows he is being led.

Within the first couple of weeks of their birth, several lamb candidates are identified by the Shepherd for the post. They should look healthy with certain strong features like good hooves and horns. The test of docility is a rather simple one, where the Shepherd touches the genitals of one of the candidates. Should the reaction be violent or semi-violent, like kicking the Shepherd with his hind legs or butting him with his horns, the Shepherd will know that this particular lamb is too aggressive to become a Mirya'. Should a lamb, after repeated tests, show no such violent reaction, he is immediately removed from his mother and starts having his milk from the Shepherd's cup or plate until he forgets his mother completely and gets attached to the Shepherd. Within the first three months of his life the lamb, in addition to a few other docile lambs, will be castrated by the Shepherd. The first will become the chief Mirya' with the others as alternatives or shadow Mirya's, should anything happen to him. The castration has two aims; the first is to cause him to develop a very large body to be respected by the other rams, and the second so that his mind will never stray to personal or sexual matters but will be wholly devoted to his leader, the Shepherd.

Incidentally, one of the most immediate problems of the Shepherd is what to do with a 'retired' Mirya'. Reasons for his possible early or even later retirement are many. However, chief among them is the fact that, due to his castration, he becomes too huge in body, too quickly, which often makes him not only slow in movement but in thinking as well. The Shepherd truly has a problem with him. You see, butchers, even at reduced prices, do not favor the purchase of a retired Mirya' – his flesh is too odorous and tough for consumption. A clever Shepherd usually 'showers' such a Mirya' with titles and attempts to sell him to other Shepherds. When all else fails, he keeps him on, until such time as he is visited by some unwelcome quests, at which time the retired Mirya' is served up as the main dish. To his favorite guests, those he likes, the Shepherd serves young tender lambs only.

The proper demeanor for a Mirya', or even for that matter a ram, appears to combine fearsomeness, respectability and as august a look as possible, since image is very important here. The ability to fool others is also immensely important. In a pasture called Italisheepia they call it 'furbo'; the image is just as important if not more so than the actual performance. A Mirya' or ram should utter the proper sounds, backed-up with a larger than usual body; and have horns that are turned backward but swaggeringly swung forward, in a sort of fearsome way that is at the same time calculated to do the least damage in case of a butting contest between the Mirya' and some other prominent ram in the flock. Three things should be remembered here. One is that the Shepherd does not mind, in fact encourages, butting contests among his rams, including their chief, the Mirya'. Secondly, he encourages such contests, or 'sporting' as far as he is concerned, as long as they do not inflict serious or visible damage on the participants. Remember, "All rams belong to the Shepherd, including the Mirya'," is a sheepular saying that describes a true-to-life situation. Every sheep in Sheepland knows that. The third is the fact that the Shepherd begins to look for a new chief ram, a Mirya', the moment that he has already chosen one. One sheepologist states that Shepherd behavior in this case is not altogether unethical. This expert asserts that from the Shepherd's vantage point the continuous stability of the system is more valuable than that of the individual Mirya' or for that matter his ideologies. This is so much so that many a Mirya' has in fact been sent to the butcher by his own friendly Shepherd. Nor should it be discounted, these prominent sheepologists state, that all sheep, rams and even Mirya's are happy to sacrifice their lives, or have them sacrificed for the

Shepherd. A prominent mulologist who has studied sheep behavior rather closely, if at the same time rather curiously, stated that it is the ambition, in fact the supreme hope of all sheep, whatever their category or station in life, to be sacrificed for the benefit or pleasure of their Shepherd. One prominent ram let it be known that his entire *raison d'être*, as well as that of his entire generation of sheep, was to end up in cooked, delectable pieces on the table of their Shepherd and his guests. Curious, yet in a way it brings to mind the saying, "Even rams are meat."

THE GOATS

No one knows for certain why the Shepherd continues to allow goats into his herd. Viewing it from the outside without having the proper data that is, no doubt, available to the Shepherd, it seems incongruous that he allows their continued and often disruptive existence. Surely they give less milk; their coarse hair, while useful in some ways, could easily be replaced by other materials; their bodies are leaner; and their meat is less in demand. All in all, they bring in less for the investment, and yet hardly a flock is without its goats, who roam often willy-nilly and seemingly always out of step with the procession. Unlike sheep they are often accused of thinking for themselves. Daring, they sometimes even demand sheep rights in accordance with a mysterious charter they love to refer to.

Why does the Shepherd keep them when he could ostensibly be rid of them? What function, if any, do they serve? Is it ordained that every flock must have its maverick goats? These and similar questions have caused nightmares to both goatologists and flock behaviorists. All in all, however, they do seem to have a definite and useful function in the life of the flock. Some sheepologists argue that the most interesting members of the flock are the goats and sheep renegades from other flocks. One prominent sheepologist stated that the renegade, or strange ewe, often becomes more important than the indigenous goats, what with her becoming the favorite of the Shepherd and the coquette of the Mirya' and other notable rams. Such is certainly contrary to sheep belief expressed in the sheepular saying, "From the mud of your country cover your face," which as a parochial attitude still expresses deep sheep-thought.

Perhaps it is because the goats have the ability to perceive, absorb, and eventually advance new ideas that some Shepherds even like them. Curiously enough, and contrary to sheepular belief, goats are also cleaner in thought and even in body than sheep. Or is it that the Shepherd likes them because of their seemingly inherent lack of discipline? Seemingly because in fact, and contrary to all appearances, goats are disciplined in their own fashion. Just remember that sheeppies and *avant garde* sheepellectuals are disciplined species notwithstanding their appearance. No creature that can produce ideas is an undisciplined creature, though his appearance may belie it. They only look undisciplined or incapable of organization. One goat expert stated flatly that it is due to their frustration and impatience with the status quo, which goats of all ages have continued to deplore, that they continue to behave the way they do. Their tails up as a sign of continued protest, unlike sheep whose tails are down, and they continue to be both exposed and uninhibited about expressing their opinions; a fact that keeps them in trouble. Like the doctor who attended so many births, delivered so many babies, observed it all from the moment of genesis, they are not inhibited in delivering their ideas. Though idea empire-builders, and dreamers, the goats continue to be undercut by the practical, well organised

Shepherd, whom they often irritate by demanding freedom for sheep thought.

In Sheepland their rebelliousness is not an innate negative goat-trait, as some superficial goatologists assert. It is much more than that, and there are many positive aspects to their nature. Historically speaking, goats have been the bearers of great ideas, the revolutionaries of every age, whose function it is to question the apparent, or seemingly apparent realities. Shepherds recognize, though perhaps unconsciously, the desperate need for goats among their flock although, consciously, they continue to deny the necessity of their existence. What respectable Shepherd, who prides himself on thinking for his sheep, would readily admit to the necessity of goat presence? Some would argue that in the mass society of recent times, especially in Sheepland, goats represent the last vestiges of individualism, initiative and innovative spirit; that in the absence of institutions, their continued existence, regardless of its seeming noxiousness to Shepherds, is of vital importance. One sheepular saying that is not current in contemporary Sheepland goes, "Goats are the yeast necessary for fermentation," while another with perhaps mild exaggeration goes, "Goats are the salt of the pasture." It is a curious innuendo, perhaps originally designed to belittle the goats, since goats are usually black while sheep are white. Is it perhaps a reversal of roles? Some goatologists think that goat faces turned black from their embarrassment at the way the Shepherd behaves, although they themselves bear no responsibility for his activities.

In peace time, the goats act as the devil's advocate, while in time of crisis they are the true defenders of sheep; gaining not only the love and admiration of the latter but the respect and recognition of the dogs. A few decades ago, a skinny but famous Mahatmagoat in Indiasheepia succeeded in liberating a huge flock of sheep, numbering at the time almost six hundred million. That particular goat was once even received at BuckingRam Palace.

In a recent study published by the Centre of Goatamalogical Studies, the theory was advanced that goats represent two basic developments. First: their ability to sustain their existence against what has often been described as terrific odds. It has been liberally documented, and the lives of notable and worthy goats throughout history demonstrate , that some goats at times have resorted to eating trash, discarded newspapers, and other refuse. There exists a famous painting in a Sheepland Pastural Gallery in one of the western pastures showing a well-known billy goat munching on a discarded tin can. Anti-goat sentiment once attempted to spread the word that this particular billy was a habitual drunk, and that the painting depicts him imbibing spirtits rather than eating. No one, nowadays, takes such slanderous allegations seriously, though this well-known painting portrays some of the anti-sheepellectual tendencies latent in most areas of Sheepland. Second: the continued desire of goats to climb, despite the basically anti-goat sentiments, and their thwarted ambitions that seem never to succeed either in their own times or in their own flock. One saying that crudely portrays their frustration goes, "There is no dignity for a goat in its own flock." Only goats that know how to please the Shepherd, his dogs or chief rams can ever hope for longer and healthier lives. By definition, goats are constantly on the mind of the organizers of the procession.

Accounting partly for this is the continued agitation of the goats themselves; in addition, somehow they can never quite succeed in blending into the scenery. Their whole demeanor, the sounds they frequently emit, their disorganized scattering all over the pasture,-never in anything resembling a procession. Their internal bickering and squabbling over often incomprehensibly fine if irrelevant points, in addition to their color, make it difficult for them to go unnoticed by the Shepherd and his dogs.

The Shepherd, while often finding them amusing, never forgets they are a constant source of nuisance and a threat to the stability of the flock. And while having them constantly surveyed by the dogs, he too personally watches over them and the dogs, at the same time. Most Shepherds believe that their biggest headache comes when dogs and goats reach some sort of understanding or cooperation. It happens at times! The Shepherd does not like to see them even peacefully co-existing with each other, and he is constantly at great pains explaining to each of them separately that the other party is conspiring against them. What with dogs' teeth and goats' brains, such a combination is indeed threatening!

Surely the reader must have realized by now that goats do have a very important role or roles in the flock. The Shepherd finds them useful not only as 'technocrats' and such, but in their capacity and ability to stir sheep imagination once in a while. He also finds them useful as negative points of refer-ence sometimes, and as positive ones at other times. Negative, as he points them out to his sheep as troublemakers and non-conformists who are constantly trying to stir up the rams; and positive when he proudly displays the least odorous ones to visiting Shepherds or dignitaries to his pasture. Some expert mulologists who find themselves frequently in sympathy with the goats think there is an interpastural conspiracy to contain them. A notable ram from a southern pasture came out on TV categorically against goats, and demanded the conclusion of interpastural treaties to contain them. The Shepherd is also keenly aware that some rams, under certain conditions, can develop goat-like behavior, which is, in his view, a catastrophe. For him a dog-ram-goat combination is a very dangerous affair indeed. It gives Shepherds nightmares to contemplate the, hopefully for them, perishable thought.

With all the above mentioned reservations, however, most enlightened Shepherds, even in the southern and eastern pastures, find goats a necessity and are willing to tolerate their existence. Some Shepherds often go to great lengths in attempting to emphasize that they belong more to the goats than to the sheep; a ruse that fools neither sheep nor goats, nor is it even acceptable to the mules. The dogs hate the very idea, what with their latest anti-goat bias. Goats, however, are certainly a welcome distraction to the Shepherd from the drab dullness of the sheep. Certainly the billy goats are often a source of headaches, but at the same time they are a source of pride for most Shepherds. No Shepherd, for instance, has ever succeeded in castrating a true billy goat, and most Shepherds think of them as sex maniacs with overwhelming ego and drive. It is noteworthy that goats and billies never walk in the procession in any kind of order, and certainly never, or very, very rarely, behind the Shepherd. Furthermore, no billy goat has ever been known to have a bell hung around his neck by the Shepherd, nor will they accept special diets, often preferring what little they scratch up for themselves to the juicy fodder the Shepherd is almost always ready to feed them. To some they seem like a no-concession pasture. It is also not unkind to state that no billy goat ever acquired status with age; on the contrary, their social status seems to deteriorate as they grow older, with Shepherds spreading the word that their odor increases in obnoxiousness. On the other hand, the status and veneration of the rams continuously advances. One wit once remarked, "Goats are invariably the scapegoats of the flock.".Martyrs? It is not a coincidence that most goats never reach maturity. Under one pretext or another the Shepherd always finds reasons to get rid of them; this, in spite of the malignant rumor that he himself advances that their flesh is smelly, tough, and not as tasty as that of sheep. Another contradiction, but who in Sheepland has the guts, the time or the inclination to research the facts and set the record straight?

THE EWES

Some remarks concerning the status and conditions of the ewes of the flock now seem to be in order. Although ewes, highly prized for their reproductive value, have in recent decades received universal suffrage, in effect their status still lags behind that of other creatures in Sheepland. Expert ewelologists have taken great pains to point out that ewe conditions have improved through pamphleteering, music sessions – even by the Shepherd himself singing the praises of ewes – and special seminars and symposia devoted to the issue of improving the status of ewes. But the fact remains that most ewes still feel grossly insecure. Also, while the cult of the ewe, the backbone of the society and the provider of future hope, has spread, in fact their status has not changed appreciably, ewes are aware that in Sheepland even the status of the rams is not so good, their lives being constantly threatened by unforeseen forces that they cannot comprehend nor control. At most, ewes feel tolerated and humored. One ewe recently remarked that whatever status they have supposedly attained is mere tokenism. Saying this, however, and then acting upon it, are two different things. Ewes are more helpless than all the other creatures in Sheepland.

Ewes too are confused by the Shepherd. He seems to be a few steps ahead of them at every bend of the road. No sooner do they think up one idea than he grasps it and immediately makes it his own. Constantly manicuring their hooves, brushing their fleece, even dyeing it in exotic colors, the ewes are ever mindful of the powers of the Shepherd and the favors he appears to shower on them. They know that these are gifts not rights. And although most ewes are happy to give up even their lambs to him, and get fleeced and milked, they are aware that they, too, like other members of the flock, have no dignity. Only through the goodness of his heart and his largesse do they acquire any privileges. Privileges that he, the Shepherd, seems to be able to withdraw at his own will. When they sometimes dare venture an opinion, they can feel the trivializing meaningful looks exchanged between the Shepherd and his rams and dogs.

In some pens in Arabisheepia, where the word for ewe is derived from the word for sin, haram, ewes are kept in segregated corrals concealed from view, sometimes even wearing what look like blinders, not allowed outside unless accompanied by a ram relative. Having any contact with or being looked upon by a ram of another flock is regarded as a dishonor to the entire flock and subject to draconian punishments. There, this behavior towards the ewe prized as producer of future generations, whose life is supposedly worth that of seven rams, is sanctioned by the Shepherd on the grounds that the ewe must be protected from all harm, including bad thoughts she might be exposed to as the result of outside exposure.

In one large far-eastern pasture, in order to control the ram-pant growth in sheepulation, laws were passed forbidding the production of more than one offspring to the union between a ewe and a ram. In a culture where rams were the offspring of preference, one can only imagine the unspeakable crimes committed against the forbidden newborn ewes to say nothing of the punishments meted out to the second offspring, regardless of gender. No wonder then, as some very prominent sheepologists conjecture, that ewes constantly look so forlorn, with droopy and watery eyes; eyes that seem to be expecting the very worst to happen at any moment.

Like the other creatures in Sheepland, ewes seem to be in continuous wonderment and awe of the Shepherd. They know not when his 'knife' will fall, nor how, nor why, their status seemingly frozen and at the mercy of the Shepherd and his alert dogs. Their ewesfulness looked upon as being mainly in the field of reproduction. This, in spite of the many leagues, liberation organisations and ewe movements for their empowerment that have formed over the past two centuries in all the pastures of Sheepland, developed and not so developed. They continue to watch, mostly helplessly, what takes place, even to themselves. The Shepherd and rams have always taken upon themselves the responsibility for 'protecting' the ewes, the implication being that they are somehow inferior, both mentally and physically, and not up to taking care of themselves.

While great strides continue to be made to change this attitude, particularly in the Super Pasture, There, the Super Shepherd and his rams are still trying to regulate, legally and on religious grounds, their reproductive activities, their major role in life. Even in pastures where ewes seem to be highly respected, attaining prominence and even reaching positions of great importance in the flock, success has come at the expense of their ewefeminity. Every ewe, however, hopes that her offspring will become a prominent ram or Mirya'.

THE MULES

Sheepland has mules too. It may be recalled that in the procession of the flock, the Shepherd is either riding on or is followed by his mount, usually a donkey or a mule. The laboring mule is a romantic figure in most cultures of Sheepland; respected and yet at the same time disdained. Because of the circumstances of their birth, most mules feel alien, and they are also made to feel this way by other creatures of the pasture. Those mules whose uncle on the mother's side is a horse take pride in the fact, which further alienates them since no one expects a mule, under any circumstances, to be proud. Some, therefore, become professional aliens, and the fact that they have no readily identifiable family or tribe, so to speak, to support them, makes them feel more alien than ever in Sheepland. In a way, some observers argue they are better off not being beholden to any family or tribe, and thus also not suffering from their history as, say, the rams or the goats do. As they do not suffer from their history, having accomplished no great feats, they worry about the future, physically sterile as they are. It is curious, however, that they love the newborn offspring of other creatures.

It has been almost three thousand years in Asheepia Minor in eastern Sheepland that the Shepherd has bred and used the mule as a beast of burden. The mule may be identified as a terminal animal in that it produces no offspring. It is a hybrid whose father usually is a donkey and whose mother usually is a mare. When the father is a horse and the mother is a jackass the result is called in English a hinny. In the eastern parts of Sheepland the latter creature is not bred, nor for that matter is it well known. One mulologist recently disclosed a third species of mule whose father is a donkey and whose mother is a cow. This expert claimed that such a species is rarely bred since it combines 'bad' traits from both the father and the mother. He also claimed it was ugly, with the prominent facial features of the cow on the body of a jackass. The whole matter goes to illustrate the difficulty in trying to ascertain mule origin. Regardless of their heritage or parentage all mules have the inferiority complex of a doomed species. They have to depend on others to be produced. They feel they are doomed, and rarely smile when some sheep might say they 'got a kick out of' a particular situation.

As with almost all other creatures in Sheepland, mules have been exploited for quite a long time. Although sterile, they remain the unsung heroes of the land, the strength of their backbones being their ticket to survival. They realize, as others do, that their continued existence in Sheepland is due to their hard labor as well as to the fact that they pose no threat whatsoever to the sheep. They bend over backwards to fraternize with and please the sheep, which in fact pleases the Shepherd immensely. Some gifted mules have been known to try to look like sheep. Such attempts are rare occurrences though. Although keeping blinders on his mule for easy direction and manipulation, occasionally the Shepherd extols their virtues and sings special songs for them, usually on the first of May, and in one western pasture in the first week of September; and as much as he hates it, the Shepherd sings some very special tunes found desirable among mules. The occasion commemorates some glorious incident in mule history. On that occasion in May, it seems, some mules took themselves seriously and attempted to establish a certain kind of fraternal commune especially for themselves in Sheepland – an unheard-of radical notion, that was so resented by Shepherds from all over Sheepland that they banded together and ruthlessly crushed the attempt. The Shepherds where worried about mule future, and some were heard muttering in disgust, "What would mules do by themselves?" In any case, hardly any of the mules is currently aware of what they, or rather their Shepherd, is celebrating. Dutifully, however, some of them don their best attire and appear for the music session of the Shepherd.

Held in the proper cultural atmosphere, in some areas in the Palace of Culture, the celebrations are usually well attended by Sheepland's dignitaries; the Shepherd, all smiles, followed by the Mirya', chief ram, other important rams and ewes of the flock; dogs of various categories wearing their finest uniforms and their latest medals and merit badges; as well as other functionaries of the pastures. They enter the premises to the sounds of martial music and much braying and bleating and stomping of hooves. The atmosphere is exceedingly friendly and gay, with every creature standing on hind legs to please everyone else. Every creature looks clean for the occasion. The Shepherd vey skillfully plays a very special tune abundant with allusions to the virtues of mulehood. A fraternal atmosphere permeates the celebrations and every creature begins to feel a true sense of achievement and camaraderie. The mules, very vulnerable and sensitive by nature, are easily touched, and their eyes water with the glee of gratitude. Some of them, especially when listening to the Shepherd, wish they had done more. A true zenith of belonging is felt when the Shepherd utters statements like, "Mules are the wave of the future," (a contradictory statement, yet it passes without notice; "Mules are the backbone of our social and economic life," "Mules are the true heroes of Sheepland," and a curious statement that goes, "One day a mule will arise in whom we shall place great trust and responsibility." The ramifications of the last statement are a bit worrisome, especially to the rams and even to some of the dogs, yet because of the spirit of the occasion it is soon forgotten.

Mules and others appreciate this generous gesture on the part of their Shepherd. His words of wisdom on that occasion festoon the halls of mule unions, publications, and in fact become the veritable slogans for next year's existence. The celebrants, in particular the mules, utter their thanks to the Shepherd. Much braying and bleating is heard and the sounds of appreciation fill the air when the Shepherd hands out badges of honor and medals to deserving and distinguished mules.

It is curious that on this day mules really enjoy themselves. Their coats shining, their small hooves – smaller than those of their father the horse – highly polished, the mules on this particular day display a spirit of camaraderie which speaks well for their well-intentioned and trusting nature. Observers of mule behavior as well as expert mulologists conjecture that their good-natured behavior on that day may relate to their physical sterility which somehow, they explain, also influences their mental as well as cultural sterility. Professor Goat Butt of More Mule University flatly states that no mule ever produced anything of cultural value. He further adds that while mules have been known to carry great burdens, and help in the construction of highways or in the building of pyramids, there has not been a single poem, book, symphony, great painting or sculpture attributed to a mule: that by definition a mule stops being a mule if he ever achieves such a feat, and then becomes something else altogether which bears little resemblance to mules.

As a class, mules have the stamina to labor and to collectively produce. As individuals, mules have been known to be intellectually and culturally bankrupt. A vicious saying of slanderous proportions, which accuses mules of being stupid and stubborn goes, 'He is as stubborn as a mule'. Professor Bullseye of the Centre for Mulistic Studies asserts that trade unions have arisen in response to mule-demand and effort. It is curious that in the western pastures these mass mule movements have been viewed with suspicion, even awe. While agreeing that individually mules are, by and large, conservative, these west range mulologists claim they become radical as a group, even acquiring a ticklish pink tint. The quiet, even con-servative, nature of the mules in the less developed areas of Sheepland is attributed to the largely repressive nature of the regimes in these areas. Western range experts also point to the immense powers given to the dogs in these areas. To further control the sometimes overfed mules, the Shepherds in these less developed areas often cause the mule to have a festering wound which keeps him busy with his pain while at the same time hoping that the Shepherd, his master, will do something about it. He does. He keeps the wound open and festering!

This is another way of saying that, regardless of which pasture you are talking about, no Shepherd can take mules for granted. The Shepherd thinks they are liable to do something at any time and often without any warning. Occasionally mules try to resist in the futile hope of asserting their rights. Thus, in addition to the increased dog power, the Shepherds are happy with developments in the technological field that can be of help to the dogs. Especially now with modern eavesdropping devices no mule can utter even a very feeble bray without being detected and reported for punishment to the Shepherd. It is not a coincidence, these experts assert, also saying that of all organizations and institutions in Sheepland, the kennel has become the most developed and organized. No wonder then, these experts explain, that mules are so well tamed and well organised in Sheepland. This in addition to the fact that the Shepherd has pulled the rug, so to speak, from under their hooves by responding to their physical demands before they are even aware they have them.

Unlike in earlier times, mules are not sent to the tannery in the event of old age, sickness or disability. In some of the pens of Sheepland certain mule unions have gained paid vacations for their members as well as health insurance. It is true that certain upper class, even bourgeois rams in some of Sheepland's pasture resent the cost of these developments; they seem to be unable to change the course of events in any appreciable manner. Rams, too, are within the jurisdiction of the Kennel whose feelers and powers seem to stretch everywhere.

It is related that even in some instances where mules have succeeded in establishing their own system, they have not been happy. One mulologist in the nineteenth century acquired a large following and was instrumental in organizing a mass mule movement that did succeed in establishing a pro-mulehood regime. Curiously enough, the mulologist was a bourgeois ram by origin and from a different pasture altogether. These facts not withstanding, the pro-mulehood movement spread to many other pastures of Sheepland, eventually banding together to establish a separate colorful bloc in eastern Sheepland, sporting a red flag. After a brief period of enforced self-quarantine, these eastern sheep pastures were 'opened up' again. Rumors still abound that even here, in this pro-mulehood 'paradise', the mules were still exploited, classes having already arisen; and rams, thought of as a class that didn't exist any more. having been liquidated in the original uprising, began to appear with frightening frequency, bringing to mind the original class structure in an order that was supposed to be classless.

A runaway ram sheepellectual, Djilram, originally part of one such pro-mulehood, condemned the development of such classes and was incarcerated and had his horns trimmed to a smaller size. It was eventually the banding together of the Shepherds of the rich western pastures that caused the collapse of this historically significant experiment of a 'mules' paradise' in Sheepland.

These developments in the various parts of Sheepland, east, west or in its rural less developed areas, have led many mulophiles and scholars to conclude that mules will always be regarded as mules by other creatures in Sheepland; that no sooner do they take off the halter and yoke of one Shepherd and his ram and dogs, than another Shepherd with his coterie – somehow unbeknownst to them at first – re-harnesses them and even while they welcome him, gets right into the saddle, holding the reins as tightly as the previous Shepherd.

In the western pastures of Sheepland, mule exploitation is no less frequent, albeit with a different approach. Here, mules are humored into thinking that they have the freedom to stop working. Ultimately a myth, of course, but mules there like to believe it.

Wherever they are, however, mules never seem to be appreciated even by the sheep, in spite of the fact that they represent the cross-fertilization of different species and cultures. They are often either dropouts from the rams or new arrivals from the pastures of the rural areas.

THE DOGS

The dog is a four-legged mammal, probably the earliest animal domesticated by man, around ten thousand years ago, and found throughout the world. The dog is a very versatile animal; essentially a domesticated wolf, it possesses a great genetic plasticity permitting the breeding and the crossbreeding of more than four hundred distinguishable breeds. With a keen sense of smell, sharp hearing and good visual capability, the dog has been found very useful to the Shepherd. It is well documented that dogs are very faithful to the Shepherd often beyond the call of duty. Many canine experts think that the symbiotic relationship between Shepherd and dog is based on a bond much stronger than material mutual benefit. It has been observed that they often anticipate the Shepherd's desires faster than he can think them up.

The dog can be trained to be formidably efficient, with eyes and ears everywhere, while even his hair may grow to become tendrils that can feel, and see, and smell even the faintest pulse of rejection or discontent.

Ancient and long forgotten viciousness, legacy of his wolf ancestry, can be recalled in an instant by the Shepherd, when the seemingly friendly and peaceful creature instantly turns into a fearless machine that can control crowds, subdue riots, sniff-out dope, drugs, even hidden weapons. "Let sleeping dogs lie," is a saying that has never been popular among Shepherds. The

Shepherd, in fact, has always tried to obliterate this saying, as he is aware that a sleeping dog is of little use. Outsiders think that the Shepherd is keen on having very alert and faithful dogs. In fact a 'good' Shepherd may require several types of dogs; regulators, manipulators, chasers, pointers, searchers, sniffers… The Shepherd has use for all of them. And use them he does!

The Shepherd locates the right types and recruits them for his service from early puppyhood. The dog often eats with the Shepherd, thus absorbing some of his intimate habits and thoughts. It is in these moments of relaxed intimacy that both understand each other and communicate. The Shepherd instills the virtues of devotion, discipline and a capacity for hardship and heroism. Such virtues are deep-rooted and it is rare – and only in certain undeveloped pastures of Sheepland where the legitimacy of the Shepherd himself is in question that dogs sometimes attempt to unseat their Shepherd. Eventually, however, and to counter this eventuality, the Shepherd sets the dogs against each other. He has certain types trained to sniff-out such bad thoughts as may occur in other types. Lately it was revealed that one Shepherd in Arabisheepia had at least nine kennels with different specializations.

The training continues with periodic check-ups and exercises. Dogs are taught to think that sheep thought is at best irrelevant, and at worst seditious and thus contrary to the interests of the Shepherd. Since their loyalty is, or should be, undivided, they cannot visualize why it is at all necessary to consult with any sheep. A sheepular saying current among the dogs of Sheepland goes, "Elections are irrelevant because they are confusing." To counter such confusion a cult is soon built around the Shepherd complete with ceremony, ritual and taboos. He becomes too distant; too difficult to approach.

Mutually, the Shepherd promotes the image created by his dogs. He never tires of associating with then. He finds countless occasions to 'show them off,' He plays a special tune for them in which much whistling is done and wind instruments are used. His elite pedigree dogs are given special food, status and privileges. On the whole, they receive a fair share – some would say more than a fair share – of the attention and love of the Shepherd. In fact, many sheep wish they were dogs; and some sheep, at times try to be.

Issue-led rather than ideology-oriented, they are mainly concerned with stability. Most dogs think that stability is an absolute necessity for any level of action, regardless of how insignificant it seems. This is why, while some are asleep, others are awake, alternating their rest periods. Not only do they watch out for what they consider 'antisocial' sheep behavior, they also watch over thought, straight and proper. Dogs tell the sheep that ideology contaminates the brain and boggles the mind. Proper thinking is clear loyalty to the Shepherd without any grey areas, and where loyalty is truly undivided. Either black or white, that is how sheep-thought should be, and no sheep worth its wool should attempt to stuff its mind with sheepellecturl trivia that may be passed on by the goats. Dogs are aware of the fact that the fundamental problem of sheep civilization has always been the attempted reconciliation between individual and social interests. The individual and social interests of the sheep, they think, are with the Shepherd and his dogs. This is what the sheep are taught.

Arguments about the silent majority, or about who protects the sheep from abuse within their own pasture, are dismissed by the dogs as irrelevant. Most dogs think that sheep are unable, in any case, to conceptualize any situation. For their own protection, they prevent them from forming even small congregations or groups that may hamper the Shepherd's procession. 'The procession must go on' is a byword among dogs that has reached the status of belief and dogma. No ripple is allowed in the flow of the procession if the dogs can help it.

In most of southern Sheepland, the dogs and Shepherds with pink faces and rosy cheeks have been replaced by locally born and bred varieties in the belief that these native ones will be more understanding, tender and merciful. Most sheep now wonder why things have not turned out the way they dreamt; the way they were told by the local Shepherds. Why has the milk soured and curdled so? Some of the goats think that the situation in fact has worsened, what with all the powers and prerogatives the dogs now have. Other experts think that the situation has worsened because the local breeds know the mentality of the sheep much better and understand their language. Being further down in the hierarchy of the pasture, the dogs are often more cruel. The reason for this is that often they feel they have to compete with the sheep. Knowing this, the Shepherd often incites his dogs to keep the sheep in a state of imbalance and fear. The dogs, on the other hand, often accuse the sheep of being bound by ropes woven from their very wool. It is partly the mistake of the sheep. All things bad are eventually blamed on them.

The goats, in fact also many sheep, wonder why there are so many breeds of dogs and why they seem to permeate everything. It seems at times that they are more important than the Shepherd himself, what with the free hand they have to watch over security, education, groups, ewes, morality and even belief sermons. They seem to be so omnipresent that the condition, while frightening, is soothing in a way. Big Shepherd is always worried about his sheep and that is nice of him, some pedigree dogs assert. Goats, however, and even some rams, are beginning to think that such a condition kills the vitality and conscience of sheep; eventually even their will and dreams. They wonder, 'What good are lethargic dreamless sheep?' The terror thus applied in degrees, often in a very sophisticated manner, nonetheless squeezes the life out of the sheep. Speaking of this condition and of the ever-creeping brutality, one Franz Fangoat spoke of the *Wretched of the Earth*. This goat ramellectual was lucky to have died young before witnessing the increasing wretchedness, the wretched of the earth getting more wretched.

One canine expert remarked that the dogs are less merciful than their Shepherd. In defense of the dogs, however, some would advance the argument that although it is true, there are reasons for it. For one, the dogs are never trained to see the totality of things, only fragments; fragments fed to them by the Shepherd as his interests dictate. Secondly, most dogs are color-blind and thus see things in black and white. One sheepular saying among them goes, "He who is not with me is against me." While there is a certain amount of sheeplore wisdom in this saying, it does tend to place most sheep at a disadvantage for it has not yet been proved with any certainty that sheep too are color blind. Thirdly, dogs are already trained for specific tasks. One expert specializing in canine behavior asserts that while certain breeds may have several thoughts at any given moment, only one thought seems to be clear at one time. They say that dogs have a one-track mind. Fourthly, since dogs are lower down the hierarchical ladder, their vehemence is usually more naked and brutal. They are taught not to be sensitive to the sight of blood nor to the sounds of pain. They live the condition each day. Efficiency, not mercy, is the stick by which they measure actions and results. Some experts think that down in the pen, where the dogs often reside with the sheep, brutality loses much of its meaning. Here the struggle for survival is an art, and the lucky sheep is the one that escapes the attention of the Shepherd. That is why sheep keep their heads down looking between their legs. They also know that survival requires the dulling of the senses. Their brains become attuned to expect the passing of this nightmare that somehow never seems to pass.

The Shepherd and his dogs impose his standards through a variety of means. Though some sheep are aware of the basic contradiction between them and their new masters, they never seem to be able to do much about it. They are taught to consume and eat more and their basically acquisitive appetite is constantly whetted. Some sheep develop certain airs of importance and begin to consume food conspicuously, often without taste.

The dogs have privileges that sheep, even the rams never hope to attain, and that is why they do not resent them. What good would it do anyway?

SHEEP AND THE INTERACTION BETWEEN NORTH AND SOUTH

Since the Second Great Conflict of the last century that took place basically in the western pastures, now called the North, the sheep of the other pastures of the world, with very few exceptions, have been given the impression that they are independent. The Shepherds of the North in fact encourage this thought among the sheep of other areas, insinuating here and there that sheep everywhere are equal. Yellow, black brown and other colored sheep at first believed this fuzzy idea and began to take themselves seriously. One of the first things they did was to shed their original wool, whatever its color or shade, and begin to don wool similar to that worn in the northern pastures. Assuredly, the Shepherds, even the sheep of the North, never took this change too seriously; sometimes they smiled, and even snickered, behind the backs of the southern sheep.

As the southern sheep took to believing seriously in ideas of sheep dignity, independence, even equality everywhere, their behavior began to change in ways that were not satisfactory to those in the northern areas who had no illusions, not serious ones anyway, about who really controls what, and where the damaging claws really are. But the behavior of southern sheep often did get out of hand, in spite of the sometimes subtle, sometimes not so subtle, often bloody lessons given to them. The truth of the matter is that while the Shepherds of the North pulled their dogs out of most areas of the South, there were still a few pastures where they settled their own sheep, whom they supplied with excellent claws and dogs. They maintained or hoped to maintain them in other ways. In the southernmost area of a dark continent, and in another area in the middle as well as in the heart of Arabisheepia, they planted terribly belligerent creatures who, while looking like sheep, acted like wolves. These wolves in sheep's clothing created new 'facts of life' and taught terrible 'lessons' to their neighboring pastures.

Once, when milk emanating from this latter pasture halted its northern flow for a very short period, loud howls were heard throughout the universe and the northern Shepherds swore vengeance. The terrible consequences can still be felt. No amount of wool produced or gathered by the sheep has been able to keep out the chill of the long night that settled over the area, nor offer protection against the long sharp claws of the proxy wolves that reside there. These have not only been provided with the latest claws and dogs, but have seemingly also been given license to attack and to sacrifice local sheep whenever they feel like it. In this particular pasture, Arabisheepia, not one sheep feels safe at night, or for that matter, during the day. Somehow the local dogs seem more ineffective with every new attack perpetrated by these embedded wolves in sheep's clothing.

But physical attacks and raw brute force have not been the only ways the sheep of the South have been kept in control. Surely the sheep everywhere, North and South, know that sheep must often be sacrificed. This they have come to accept from historical experience. The sheep have also ruminated over the thought that, though all religions teach love, none has succeeded in protecting them from the Shepherd or even from each other. Sheep are always preoccupied, or made preoccupied, with their daily tasks like growing wool and producing milk and, in some cases, even their flesh for others.

"These ideas are too wooly," thought one ram, "we must try exploring some of the ways devised by the North to control the other pastures." Chief among these was the novel way of getting them into debt. The economics, not only the politics of the matter, somehow always worked to the disadvantage of the southern pastures and most of them sank deeper and deeper into penury. At the gatherings of the southern Shepherds, their northern 'brethren' listened with a pretence of sympathy and seriousness to their complaints, bleatings and 'demands'. Somehow little changed afterwards, and the weighty, often fat southern sheep, with interests in the North, were always outweighed by the slim muscular sheep of the North. Balanced ecology: that is what it is, making true the saying adopted by the wolves, "May the wolf survive while the sheep flourish." Only a wolf would say that. No wonder the southern sheep have watery eyes. In fact the northern Shepherds provided a very impressive arena for debate in one of the major pens of the only Super Pasture. This United Pastures Organization, built like a high and mighty wailing wall, was as it turned out, of great service to the northern pastures. It served as a place where the attention of the southern sheep could be diverted from what was really going on elsewhere, while continuing to give false hope to them that something would be done for them sometime in the misty future – thus proving beyond doubt the saying, "Hope prolongs agony." Here, the southern pastures never tired of passing resolutions in their favor, which were mostly politely ignored by the North; a state of affairs that eventually gave rise to the sheepular saying, "What does it matter how many resolutions the sheep pass if the wolf remains of a contrary opinion!"

EPILOGUE

Following the Great Conflict and the subsequent retreat of the pink-faced Shepherds, are the Shepherds who appeared in southern Sheepland any better? Or to put it another way: are the sheep better off right now under the native Shepherds?

But then, have the pink-faced Shepherds really retreated or have they merely changed tactics? It is true that their dogs were removed from their Kennel bases in most areas of the south pastureland after the Second Great Conflict; but it is just as true that they are ever ready to control the sheep here either by remote control tactics, or by carrying out preemptive attacks against supposed errant Shepherds and their sheep. The one Super Shepherd of a western pasture – since the collapse of a once great Super Pasture of pinkish color, now called the North – recently asserted that no other Shepherd anywhere must be allowed to arise who can even hint at a threat to his divinely inspired Shepherdhood or the sole supremacy of his pasture. It is as if he himself has metamorphosed into a top dog of unusual powers that can sniff out and crush a threat before it happens. The southern sheep remain truly confused nowadays even about geography; how is it that the area once called the west is now called the North, and in Arabisheepia they wonder how the Red danger turned Green so suddenly!

This doctrine of preemptive action that the Super Shepherd emphasized is designed to promote the further equality and sheepocracy of the sheep in whatever pasture they may be. However sheepologists, mulologists and goatologists of various disciplines of knowledge, especially in dog behavior, opined that the gilded rhetoric of this Super Shepherd had nothing to do with his real intentions. In one particular instance in the southern areas of Sheepland, rich with a dark oily substance, this Super Pasture has developed a long lasting relationship with an implanted alien pasture here, and fattened its Shepherds and sheep to most unusual proportions. The Super Shepherds of the West not only supported but also fought on behalf of this alien pasture without any reservations, sometimes even if it was – as some goatologists thought – against their own interests. These goatologists therefore were led to think that while the pink-faced Shephreds and their dogs may have appeared to have withdrawn from the South, in fact they only changed tactics, and that the resources of these areas will remain – through one tactic or another – for the benefit of the North, its sheep and shepherds.

*　*　*

Generally, however, the Sheep are not asking for rights any more. They have lost hope that the Shepherd will do them much good, and all they wish for is that he refrains from doing them further harm. They see prosperity but they are never sure of the future. They have come to dread the cold silent nights when, in many areas of Sheepland, some of them disappear without a trace. Few sheep dare to ask what happened.

These chilly thoughts rarely occur to most sheep, covered as they are with so much wool. Nor does the Shepherd care to let them know what is going on. A popular saying among shepherds goes, "The woollier the thoughts of sheep, the better it is for the Shepherd." Even the sheep themselves never notice what is happening to them, which in essence goes to demonstrate the resilience of sheep and their capacity to endure.

In taking in the whole scene at a glance, however, the outside observer realizes that things are not as quaint as they look. For one, misery and abject servitude are never quaint nor palatable; they do something to the perpetrator as well as to the victim. Secondly, there is, or should be, a limit to the use of such Shepherd tactics, because the continued use of terror eventually destroys the Shepherd himself. It depersonalizes and dehumanizes him whether he knows it or not. Thirdly, the art of Shepherdhood is the art of judging the limits of force, and a true Shepherd must always search for new horizons and new frontiers to expand his sheep's welfare. Also, their welfare depends on heeding their wishes at least some of the time. As one goatologist once remarked. "You can fool all of the sheep some of the time, and some of the sheep all of the time, but you cannot fool all of the sheep all of the time." Surely no sheep can argue or think unwoolly thoughts with so many dogs hanging around and snapping at their heels. And while the Shepherd may subordinate his sheep, they in turn influence him in numerous ways. Unless he learns to respect them, their meekness and sheepishness and weakness will, like water, ultimately engulf and choke him. Fourthly, while sheep listen attentively to the Shepherd's musical sessions, they listen to what is not being played as well as to what is being played. They figure that here is the grey area where some of their rights may be found.

In the southern pastures, outside observers note that the broken dreams, the yearnings and the hopes of so many cannot forever be thwarted. The procession, though it may look orderly, is indeed an unhappy and a frustrated one. The seeming order is not really order, but in fact mere lack of lawlessness wanting to be unleashed; once unleashed it can be a scourge to the pasture. These woolly thoughts, while rarely occurring to most sheep, do occur on occasion. In the absence of proper institutions – except the Kennels, which not only survive but seem to proposer – and in the absence of proper channels to change things, the reaction, when it sets in, is a destructive one. The goats, who seem to be the least orderly creatures in the pasture, are currently wondering: is this disorder a permanent state of affairs and is it here to stay?

> 'Like sheep, most human beings,
> Wherever their pasture, are entrapped
> by socio-economic and political forces
> they do not understand, fathom,
> nor have control over.'

OF SHEEP AND SHEPHERDS IN THE AGE OF TRUMP

The erratic and unusual behavior of President Donald Trump, and his explosion onto the world scene brings to mind a book I wrote many years ago called *Sheepland*. In that book I wrote: "Like sheep, most human beings wherever their pastures, are entrapped by socioeconomic and political forces they do not understand, fathom, or have control over. A statement that supports the assertion made by Jean-Jacques Rousseau that: 'Man is born free, and everywhere he is in chains…'" Later I added, "Mostly, the tethers that keep man or sheep in their situation are unseen."

Life for the average sheep is basically the same in all pastures though the more clever Shepherds in the western and northern pastures have devised ingenious governing systems giving their ordinary sheep the impression that they actually have rights and that they can elect their rams to legislative and even executive positions. The drums and flutes of these Shepherds aided by their ever-present central sniffing agencies have actually convinced most sheep that they are truly free and equal, notwithstanding the fact that only the top 1% of rams in their flock control 99% of the wealth and food of their pasture.

The Shepherd, however he structures the machinery of his control, is omnipotent and goes to great lengths to keep his flock in a state of anxiety, uncertainty and fear. Aided by his propaganda machine; his flutes, pipes, and drums and supported by his ever vigilant Dogs, whose duty is, supposedly, to protect his flock's pasture from other encroaching Shepherds and their Dogs, the Shepherd is well aware of how to manipulate the affairs of his flock, convincing them that he has their best interests at heart and that this strict control is for their own good.

The Shepherd-in-Chief of the most important and powerful flock in Amerisheepia is quite adept at controlling his sheep, making them believe their powerful Kennel with its Central Sniffing Agency can do practically anything, anytime and anywhere without regard for what other Shepherds, even in neighboring western pastures and their flocks may feel or think about it. His constant trumpeting of fake news and false information has encouraged most of his sheep to hate all other sheep, particularly those of other colors, promising to: "Make his pastures white again." The faint bleats of protestation from some of his flock, including even some rams, have not been able to change his course which seems to have convinced other western Shepherds to follow in his path of hatred of all non-white sheep everywhere.

In many pastures in Eurosheepia, the breakdown of the façade of sheepocracy and sheepishness has been brutal; often witnessing the expulsion of refusheep of color, even allowing them to drown in the sea. This right-shank, neo-Nazisheepism and Fascisheepism trend has been camouflaged by the acronym, 'sheepulism'. In a way, many of the goats of the developing pastures, non-white in color, while condemning this unsheeply, unsheepish behavior are not so unhappy about it since it shows the true, often brutal behavior of the Shepherds of the North and other western pastures: This is especially true in the case of one Zioflock who claim to be 'chosen' who, though geographically planted in a wouthern pasture, Palisheepia, having forcefully and brutally removed the existing flock and still keep most of those who didn't escape in pens, heavily guarded by vicious dogs, in their very own pasture. Their false claim to be part of the northern pastures is even strongly supported and defended by the Shepherds of western and Euro pastures. This geographic Orwellian double think which has been rejected by all non-white sheep of the Grand Pasture, has been accepted by most shepherds of the Western pastures, especially among the Zio-evangelisheep of Amerisheepia. Their Zio-Shepherd-in-Chief, ignoring all historical logic and interpastural law, and the hue and cry and bleating of sheep, rams and even shepherds of far flung pastures, recently proclaimed the Holy Capital of Palisheepia as the capital of Zio-Israelosheepia.

The style of this new Zio-Shepherd-in-Chief of Amerisheepia coupled with his extreme hubris have thrown not only the sheep but the Shepherds, Rams and even goats of all the Western pastures into utter confusion and chaos; no longer certain of what to believe or where they belong.

...and thus continues,

    for the foreseeable future,

        the procession of the flocks.

ABOUT THE AUTHOR

Dr. Kamel S. Abu Jaber (1932–2020) received his PhD from Syracuse University and did a postdoctoral programme in Oriental studies at Princeton.

Following an academic career in the United States, he returned to Jordan to pursue an extensive academic career as well as a political career becoming Minister of Economy in 1973, Minister of Foreign Affairs in 1991, heading the joint Jordanian-Palestinian delegation to the Madrid Peace Conference. He also served as Senator to the Jordanian Parliament. Other held posts include: Director of Jordan University's Center for Strategic Studies; Director of Queen Alia Social Welfare Fund; Director of the Jordanian Institute of Diplomacy; President Higher Council for Media; President, Royal Institute for Interfaith Studies; President of Higher Council for Media; President Jordan Institute for Middle Eastern Studies.

An internationally recognised scholar, Dr. Kamel S. Abu Jaber has written many articles and books. Among his most notable books: *The Arab Ba'ath Socialist Party* (1966) and *The Palestinians: People of the Olive Tree* (1993).